STUDENT STUDY GUIDE

PURE FLIX PRESENTS

A HAROLD CRONK FILM

GOD'S NOT DEAD 2

WHO DO YOU SAY I AM?

BY RICE BROOCKS

FOREWORD BY SEAN MCDOWELL

OUTREACH®

God's Not Dead 2 Student Study Guide

Published by Outreach, Inc. Colorado Springs, CO 80919
www.Outreach.com

ISBN: 9781942027300

Cover Design by Tim Downs
Interior Design by Alexia Garaventa
Written by Rice Broocks
Edited by Tia Smith

Printed in the United States of America

CONTENTS

FOREWORD
BY SEAN MCDOWELL

Have you ever been challenged in your faith? Have you ever been asked a tough question about God or the Bible that you weren't ready to answer? In high school, I took a trip to visit a friend in the Midwest. My flight home was delayed by four hours, and so I was stuck in the airport all morning—not how I wanted to spend my day!

As soon as I got the news about my delay, I saw a young man behind me who was on the same flight. Could this be an opportunity? Should I share my faith with him since we're stuck in the same place all morning? As much as I would like to impress you with my spiritual courage, here's what I remember thinking: *God, I'm really tired and need a break. If You want me to share with him, have him sit by me on the plane.* And so I went about my business.

When the delay was over and we finally boarded the plane, I took my seat in 9A. Then I saw the young man walking down the aisle. Where would he sit? I know it sounds crazy, but he sat right next to me in 9B. I was both stunned and convicted. Whether this was truly divine intervention or mere coincidence, I figured I better start talking about Jesus!

We had a great conversation, but he quickly started pressing me to defend my beliefs. He wanted to know if the Christian claims were credible. I remember him looking me right in the eyes and saying something like, "How do you really know the Bible is true? What about all the contradictions? Do you really think a dead man can come back to life? Hasn't science disproven this?"

I was stunned once again, but for a different reason. While I had some initial answers to his questions, I totally failed to defend my faith in a compelling manner. I felt defeated, devastated, and disappointed. Nevertheless, as Rice Broocks points out in lesson 3 of this study, *failure isn't final*. I was disappointed and upset, but it also gave me greater resolve to be ready the next time someone challenged my faith.

This is why the apostle Peter said, *"But in your hearts honor Christ the Lord as holy, always being prepared to make a defense to anyone who asks you for a reason for the hope that is in you; yet do it with gentleness and respect" (1 Peter 3:15, ESV)*. In the original Greek, the word for "defense" is *apologia*, which means giving reasons, answers, and an explanation for our beliefs. Defending the faith, what we call apologetics, is not merely for teachers, pastors, and parents; it's a command for every believer regardless of age. That's right. As Christians, we are called to be ready with an answer for why we believe as we do.

So, how would *you* have done in my shoes? Honestly, can you give good reasons why you think the Bible is true or why Jesus was resurrected? My guess is that you can't. Before you get defensive, let me explain. One of my favorite presentations to give at churches, camps, and schools is what I call "The Atheist Encounter." The audience typically knows I am a Christian, but I begin the presentation by putting on my "atheist glasses," which transform my worldview into that of an outspoken atheist. I challenge the audience to ask good questions and defend their faith, and then I do my best to respond as an atheist might.

With a few exceptions, the vast majority of people (students included) cannot offer a reasonable defense of their faith. I have done my atheist role-play before *tens of thousands* of Christians, and it is rare to find a knowledgeable and articulate Christian who can defend his or her beliefs. My point is not to beat up on Christians. I am one! But if you cannot defend your faith, you will be less likely to share your faith, less likely to live your faith with boldness, and more likely to disengage from the church as you get older.

Here is the bottom line: As a student, one of the most important things you need to learn is to defend your faith with clarity and conviction. And this is why I am so thrilled that you are going through the *God's Not Dead 2 Student Study Guide*. But watch out because this study is unlike any you've done before!

Sometimes youth ministry involves eating pizza, listening to brief motivational talks from the Bible, and sharing your personal story. While each of these certainly has its place (especially if the pizza is Hawaiian!), Jesus has called us to so much more. He told His disciples to pick up their crosses and follow Him (Matthew 16:24). Essentially, Jesus was telling His followers that if they truly wanted to follow Him, they needed to prepare to die. Following Jesus may cost you everything. *"If the world hates you,"* claimed Jesus, *"know that it has hated me before it hated you" (John 15:18, ESV).* Following Jesus is the most rewarding life possible, but it comes at a price.

You can expect three things from this study:

1) **You will be challenged to *think*.** While we hope you enjoy this study, our biggest goal is that you learn to think more deeply about your faith. You will be challenged not only to love God with your heart and soul but also with your *mind* (Mark 12:28–31). Get ready, because we're going deep!

2) **You will learn to defend your faith *graciously*.** We are going to tackle some of the toughest questions that Christians face, such as "Why does God allow evil?" and "How can a dead man come back to life?" But you will also be equipped to share these truths in a manner that is both gracious and kind (Colossians 4:6).

3) **You will learn how to share your faith *naturally.*** Let's face it—talking about Jesus with unbelievers can sometimes be awkward and intimidating. One reason many of us don't share our faith is that we don't know how. Yet as you will learn in this study, it is both possible and rewarding to share your faith if you simply learn how.

There has never been a more important time for a study like this. The days when Christianity was held in cultural esteem are done. Christians who really see the Bible as true are increasingly seen as bigoted, intolerant, and hateful. And some Christians, as you can see in the case of Grace in *God's Not Dead 2,* even pay a price for their faith.

And yet rather than despair, this is an opportunity for Christians to shine. Jesus is God and He is in control. The question is whether we will follow Him no matter the cost. I'm in. Are you?

Sean McDowell, PhD
Biola University

INTRODUCTION

WHO DO YOU SAY I AM?

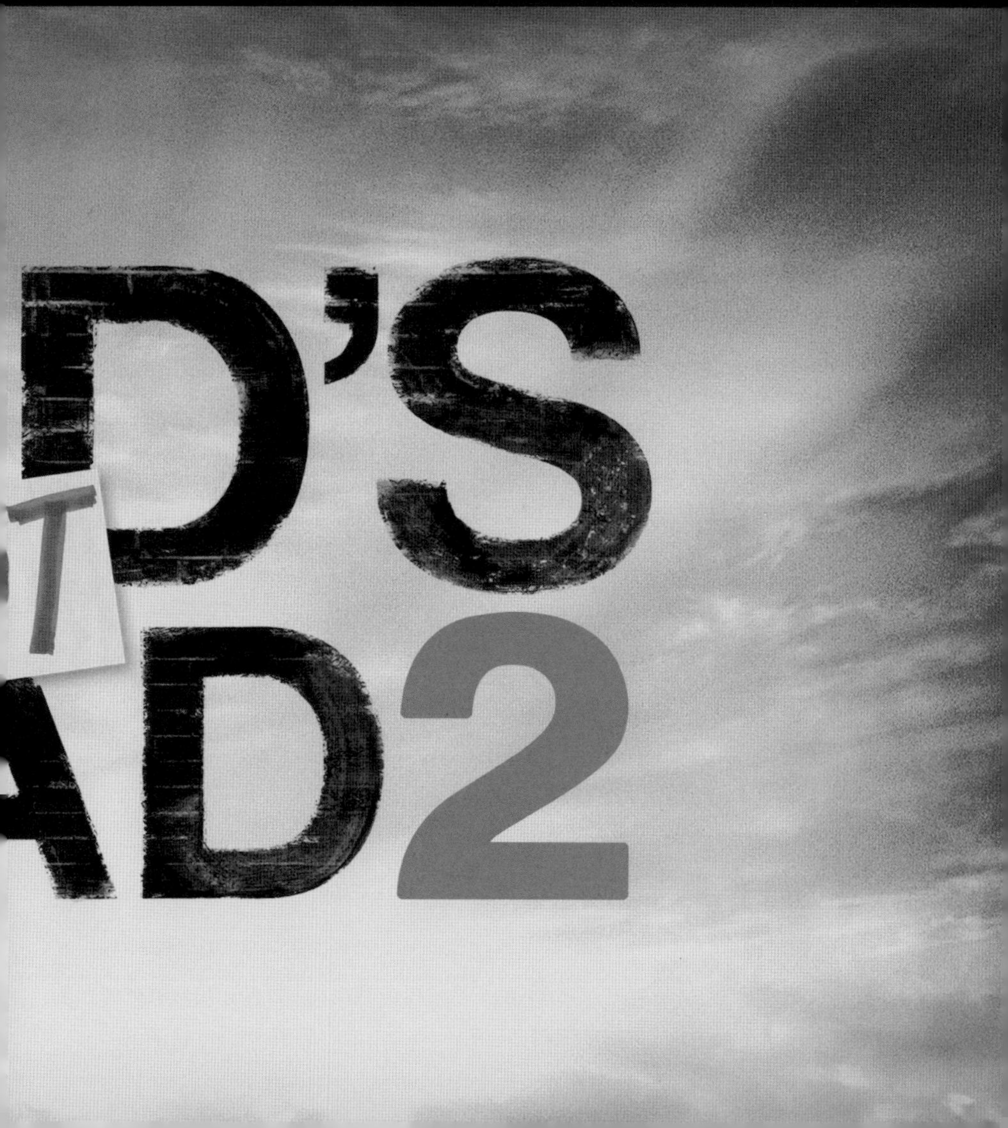

A few years ago, I wrote a book called *God's Not Dead: Evidence for God in an Age of Uncertainty*. I was deeply troubled by the reports of young people abandoning the Christian faith once they left high school and attended college. Studies showed they were being influenced by a rising chorus of skeptical voices from pop culture and vocal atheists claiming there was no evidence for God's existence. The goal of the book was to give a clear presentation of the evidence for God from science, philosophy, history, theology, and personal experience.

A friend of mine heard about the book I was writing and introduced me to Pure Flix, a faith-based movie company that expressed interest in bringing this drama to the big screen. They flew to Nashville, where I live, and we discussed the challenge that people of faith face on the university campus. It was deeply encouraging to hear their desire to do something that could give a response to the voices of atheism and unbelief and help people of all ages gain the solid footing needed for a real and lasting faith. It was an amazing thing to see those conversations and the evidence I was writing about turned into a movie called *God's Not Dead*. It became a box-office success in the United States and was shown literally around the world.

Even before the first movie was completed, there was discussion about another movie that would tackle the issue of the existence of the historical Jesus. I embarked on another writing journey with a book called *Man, Myth, Messiah: Answering History's Greatest Question*. It has resulted in the sequel, *God's Not Dead 2*. The story line is compelling, and the movie itself is based on true-to-life events and challenges that are happening in America with increased frequency and intensity.

It's becoming glaringly apparent that any reference to the Christian faith in the public square is unwelcome. This has had an enormous impact on the values and beliefs of an entire generation of young people (that's you!). Although there are many theories that try to explain this decline, one of the primary reasons we have discovered is *they don't believe the Gospel story is really true.* This has less to do with the skeptics presenting real evidence against the truth of the Christian faith and more to do with the unfounded and untrue attacks hurled against believers to dissuade them with mockery and ridicule.

In many countries of the world, Christians are *assaulted* for their beliefs; in America, they are *insulted* out of their faith.

Our response? *Real faith isn't blind.* It is based on evidence, not merely subjective experience. Christianity answers the deepest questions of the heart *and* mind. Tragically, if those answers aren't known, it means there is no foundation that undergirds someone's faith. Merely having religious traditions isn't enough. I bet you have known people who seemed to be solid believers but were blown away when they faced intellectual challenges to their faith. As Scripture warns, "*My people are destroyed from lack of knowledge*" *(Hosea 4:6).*

While Bible studies and youth activities abound, there must be a clear understanding of the Gospel and an unwavering conviction of its truth. There is no way you can boldly live for Christ without a solid foundation that can withstand the challenges of skepticism and unbelief. In the movie *God's Not Dead 2*, a high school teacher, Grace Wesley, mentions Jesus Christ in a public classroom and then quotes His words written in the Gospels. She is suspended from her job and faces a lawsuit for her actions. Her crime? Simply referring to the words of the most influential person who ever lived. She finds herself having to take a stand, which could result in her losing her job. Her type of courage in the face of opposition is an inspiration to all of those who are being pushed, intimidated, and told to keep their faith locked up and far away from any public expression. Her boldness helps point people to the truths of the Gospel. This shouldn't just happen in the movies.

Our deepest desire is that through these *God's Not Dead* films, books, and study guides there will be a multitude of believers who will become defenders of the faith and take the kind of stand Grace took. The story line of *God's Not Dead 2* includes a young girl named Brooke Thawley, who has lost her beloved brother and is searching for hope in the face of this family tragedy. Her parents are skeptics and simply want to "move on" rather than deal with the issues of eternity and life after death. Brooke's struggle leads her to her high school history teacher Grace Wesley, who shares her faith in Jesus with Brooke. This search for answers is a common theme in the movie.

Martin, the college student from China we met in the first movie, brings a list of 147 questions to Pastor Dave for answers.

Amy, the skeptical reporter from the first movie, discovers she's been healed from cancer and dedicates her writing to chronicle her search for God.

Grace, the high school teacher, is searching for the reasons why she is facing such persecution and why she feels abandoned by God in her struggle.

All of these types of struggles are common today as people search for answers to the pressing questions that arise from a dramatically shifting moral and political landscape. The real question now is: Whose words should we trust?

In the movie, Grace is called to the witness stand and asked to reveal how God had actually spoken to her. She reluctantly explains how she believes God asked her a question through a church sign she encountered: "Who do you say I am?" I call this "history's greatest question" in the book *Man, Myth, Messiah*.

Answering this question will be the defining decision of your life: Was Jesus a man, a myth, or the Messiah?

If He was just a man, we can admire Him.

If He was a myth, we can be entertained and even inspired by these heroic tales just as we are when we watch *The Avengers* or some other superhero story.

But if He is the Messiah, that means we should follow Him with all our heart, soul, mind, and strength. It also means that His words are the ones we can trust.

If there is no clear moral authority, then we are left with the schoolyard challenge, "Says who?"

The loss of faith we have described has left masses of

people searching for meaning and purpose like never before. It is impossible to ignore the spiritual hunger in the human soul. In fact, people will eat whatever people can find to try to meet this need. Eventually people will eat dirt if they get hungry enough.

This presents us with an unprecedented opportunity to share the truth and hope that Christ offers. Tragically, at the time when hearts and minds are most open to look again to God for answers, God's people are not prepared to take advantage of this massive need. It is our prayer that you will come to the place of confidence in answering the great question the way Grace does in the movie.

"You are the Messiah, the Son of the living God" (Matthew 16:16).

LESSON 1

SEARCHING FOR ANSWERS

KEY VERSE

"And without faith it is impossible to please God, because anyone who comes to him must believe that he exists and that he rewards those who earnestly seek him." —*Hebrews 11:6*

MOVIE QUOTE

Walter Wesley: "Atheism doesn't take away the pain, it just takes away the hope."

MOVIE CLIP

Grace and Brooke at a coffee shop talking about Brooke's brother's death. Grace reveals that she looks to Jesus.

WARM-UP QUESTIONS

1) What is the biggest question (most difficult or challenging) that people have about God?
2) What has happened to you to make you search for God?

INTRODUCTION

The world is getting smaller. Technology has brought us so close together that something that happens in the Middle East is instantly known in Middle Tennessee. It seems that all news has become "breaking news." As Christians, we are alive at the most dramatic and dangerous moment in human history. Sometimes, the outlook can become so bleak that even the most faithful believer can lose hope. We must not only have enough courage and faith for ourselves, but for our neighbors and friends as well.

Sooner or later someone close to you will find themselves in a personal crisis. Many suffer in silence, while others let the world know on Facebook or Instagram. As believers, we rarely see these critical moments in life coming until they arrive. They seem to happen suddenly. That's why this movie weaves many different stories together of people who are facing different challenges and shows how faith in God helps them get through the storms. As I got to know many of the actors in the movie, it was fascinating to hear how they seemed to identify with the struggles portrayed by the characters they played.

The issue of personal faith lived out in the public arena, which is the story line of the movie, will only get bigger as the years go by. What people believe affects more than just them. That's why it is crucial we have a faith that can stand up to any challenge. As you should know, not all beliefs are equal. In America, people should have freedom to believe, regardless of their religion. But the real question isn't just a person's *right to believe* but whether what they *believe is right.* Jesus promised that we would know the truth and the truth would set us free (John 8:32). This is the kind of freedom we should pursue and consider our most valuable treasure.

1. THE PROBLEM

The greatest question people have when it comes to faith relates to the problem of pain and suffering. Whether it's senseless acts of violence or personal pain and loss, it is the elephant in the room during most discussions about God and faith.

The biggest question you will hear again and again on campus or from people you talk to about God or spiritual things is, "Why do bad things happen?"

That's because pain and suffering are everywhere. The images we are bombarded with in the media are at times like those in horror movies.

It appears that evil has no limits.

The universal cry is, "Can anything be done to stop it?"

If God is all-powerful, why doesn't He do something? The hope of this study is to show that God has already done something. In fact, the message of what God has done is so incredible it is called the Gospel or the Good News!

To fully understand what this means, we must step back a moment and look at the big picture. As the key verse at the beginning states, "*Anyone who comes to [God] must believe that he exists.*" While skeptics talk about the problem of evil when expressing doubts about God, in reality, there are far more problems for them trying to explain the universe without God.

That's why the first movie *(God's Not Dead)* gave an overview of the evidence for God. This was done primarily in the three classroom scenes.

The fact that the universe had a beginning is a huge problem for atheists to explain. How could something come from nothing? The fact that the universe began (just as Genesis 1:1 states) was not believed by science until the beginning of the twentieth century. From Aristotle to Einstein, scientists claimed the universe was eternal, with no beginning. There is no question now that the universe began. If it began, then there had to be a First Cause.

Another problem for skeptics is the origin of life. Evolution only tells you what happens once you have life; it can't explain the origin of the first cell. The complexity of living things points to an Intelligent Designer. Just as you see the evidence of intelligence in the books or texts you read, there is enormous information in the simplest of living cells that points to an Intelligent Designer.

Have you ever received a pocket text of random letters? You can instantly tell it was constructed by accident (maybe the person sat on their phone). If you receive a normal text that makes sense, you know there was a person behind the message. How much more if you see a sentence three billion letters long—the information present in our DNA!

Then there is the issue of the origin of morality. We know good and evil exist, but the problem for the skeptic is determining where these concepts (good and evil) come from. If there is no God, how can there be any such thing as evil? As the famous Russian writer Dostoevsky wrote, "If there is no God, then all things are permissible."

Yes, there is the problem of pain and suffering. But if there is no God, then that's just the way the world is. Charles Darwin called it "survival of the fittest."

Though it seems like this is how the world operates, all of us know it's not the case when it comes to human beings. We are not just animals, programmed to survive at all costs. It's true that there is nothing more universally common than selfishness and self-centeredness. At the same time, there is nothing more universally despised when we see it in others.

Could it be that we have misunderstood the real problem?

The real problem of pain is how to explain it and find hope if there is no God.

That's why the statement quoted in the movie from the *God's Not Dead* book is true: "Atheism doesn't take away the pain, it just takes away the hope."

The fact that God exists means we can be sure that there are answers. When you open a puzzle, it seems that there must be some missing pieces. Yet eventually, piece by piece, they come together. That brings us to the next key truth we must embrace: We are called to search.

2. THE SEARCH

The reality of pain and suffering has produced a void, resulting in despair in people's lives. This is the case in the movie with Brooke, the high school student who lost her brother. Many times, people try to mask their pain by simply giving themselves over to distractions. Some search for riches, fame, or attention, while others give their focus to anything they can to try to ease the pain.

If we can escape from these traps, our search for answers can become meaningful and not another dead end. Remember, *because God exists, our search for Him will not be in vain.*

God has given us enough evidence of His existence to make our search for Him a reachable goal. The good news is that God has come to us in the form of a man, Jesus

Christ. He desires to bring us the help and the hope we long for. That's why in the next lesson we will examine the evidence for the Jesus of history. For now, we are looking at the importance of our searching for God with all our heart and mind. When something important or valuable is lost, you will stop everything to locate what's missing.

If you are running from God and show up at church on a Sunday morning or at a study group examining a Christian movie, well, you're not doing a very good job. In other words, the fact that you are here demonstrates that you are searching!

In the movie, Brooke is searching for answers. "What happened to my brother?" She is asking if there is any hope beyond death. She asks, "Why do my parents simply ignore the pain by trying to move on?"

She isn't satisfied with the shallow answers others have given her. These events have started her on a journey to find the truth.

It's comforting that in real life (not just in the movies) God gives us clues to help us in this search.

First, we are promised, *"Ask and it will be given to you; seek and you will find; knock and the door will be opened to you" (Matthew 7:7).* We are promised from the beginning that our sincere search will not be in vain.

Second, Christianity not just welcomes inquiry but requires it: *"Love the Lord your God with all your heart and with all your soul and with all your mind and with all your strength" (Mark 12:30).*

We don't come to God *against* reason but *through* it.

Furthermore, Scripture says that God has given enough evidence of His existence through the world He created (Romans 1:19–20). That means science and faith are not at odds—faith and reason are friends not foes.

That's why we say, "Real faith isn't blind."

Most significantly, Christianity stands or falls on an historical event: the resurrection of Jesus Christ. Jesus came to give us the ultimate evidence of God's existence, up close and personal.

Because God is personal, He cares about us and has promised to reward us for diligently seeking Him.

3. THE HELP

One of the great privileges of life is to help others. The fact that God calls us to be involved in other people's lives makes sense. Sharing your faith in Christ is really spreading hope and offering spiritual help to others.

We have been sent by God to love others. Our neighbors gather for relationships at bars, sporting events, and so on. They show that nothing is more important than relationships with others. This is a need God has sent us to fulfill in others. That's why He commanded us to love our neighbors as ourselves (Matthew 22:39).

I can remember my search for God while in my third year of college. I went to church, read the Bible, and looked for answers watching ministers on TV. The more I searched, the farther away God seemed to be. How could my search for God be taking me away from Him? It was primarily because the people around me (my friends) were not on the same path I was trying to be on. Every step I would take away from God, they were there to encourage me in my wrong choices.

This pattern came to a dramatic end when I met a student named Greg. His boldness for Christ was contagious. He began to help me open the Bible and understand it. It is because of his help I am writing this today. He took the time to listen to my questions and help me make some good, practical decisions about how to avoid the things that could sabotage my new faith. With the help of some other new friends like him, my search for God began to make sense. I came to the place of faith and confidence in a matter of weeks. Greg is still my friend thirty years later. I will always be indebted to him for his help.

We need the help of others in this search for God. Once we have found the answers that bring us life and peace, we need to be ready to help others.

In *God's Not Dead 2*, the opposing lawyer makes this critical point. Brooke would have probably not become a Christian without the help of her teacher Grace Wesley. What a profound scene when the fact that her words of encouragement made a real difference was brought out in the courtroom!

In real life, there are literally millions of people who are in the process of reconsidering their faith in God. With this many in the balance, it is crucial that we be there to help them make a decision based on all the facts. Sadly, it's usually the skeptical voices people hear. The primary reason for this absence of the Christian perspective is that most believers aren't prepared to give the reasons for the hope they have. They may know the verse, "*Always be prepared to give an answer to everyone who asks you to give the reason for the hope that you have. But do this with gentleness and respect*" *(1 Peter 3:15)*, but it's the reasons we need to know, not just the verse. It's worth repeating again and again: It's time to get ready!

4. THE ANSWERS

It's important to keep in mind that no one has *all* the answers . . . only God has that kind of knowledge. While we are called to give the reasons for our faith, there are times I have to say to others, "I don't know." When this happens, it serves as motivation for me to study and learn so I can be ready when the same question is asked in a future discussion with someone.

It's also important to realize we don't have to have all the answers before we can come to Christ. I sure didn't—I had even more questions *after* I became a Christian. The joy of serving the Lord has been the excitement of learning and growing in the knowledge of the Truth.

When I became a Christian in my third year at university, my older brother, who was in law school and was an atheist, came home to talk me out of my faith. He had announced to his friends that he was "going home to get his little brother out of this 'born-again thing.'" He came prepared with lots of questions and objections. I listened intently and then gave my responses. The very weekend he tried to talk me out of my faith, my brother was baptized. I'll never forget him saying to me with a bewildered look on his face, "You haven't answered all my questions, but I think I was asking the wrong questions."

Today my brother Ben is an attorney in Austin, Texas, and a dynamic witness for Christ.

This brings up another important point. In helping others in their journey, we actually don't lead with the answers. We start by asking questions and listening to them first. It's amazing what you will hear when you do this. Otherwise, we might find ourselves answering questions they aren't asking.

For the most part, Jesus didn't give answers to people unless they were ready to hear them.

This is an important lesson to understand before we get into the subject of evidence (in the next lesson).

We don't want to use the truth about God or the evidence for His existence as a club to hit people. We are called to be reconcilers and healers. We are called to give the reasons for our faith, but in doing this we must have gentleness and respect—the forgotten part of 1 Peter 3:15.

This involves listening and not being quick to tell what we know and believe. If we *listen carefully* to others, they will reveal the issues or problems they are dealing with. Don't be discouraged if you have failed at this approach. As we get in the habit of helping others with the issues of faith and doubt, we will become more confident in our speaking as well as more compassionate.

5. THE HOPE

Hope is like oxygen for the soul. Without it, we seem to suffocate like a fish out of water. The Bible speaks of "*the God of hope*" *(Romans 15:13)*. It also talks about *"the hope held out in the gospel" (Colossians 1:23)*. The Gospel provides the ultimate answers that we need about God and ourselves. This is so important that we have devoted an entire lesson to it in this study (lesson 4). For now, we want to emphasize the hope that the Gospel brings.

It provides us the hope that we are loved in spite of our weaknesses, mistakes, and sins. So many times these things are like weights around us when we are trying to swim. Knowing that God loves us can be a source of enormous hope and encouragement.

There is the hope that He is aware of our struggles and our fears. God isn't detached from our circumstances. In Christ, He became a man and took upon Himself our pain at the cross (Isaiah 53:3–5).

The Gospel also provides us the hope that when this life ends, it's not the end of our existence. The thought of death can bring the strongest and most intelligent person to their knees. It can fill us with despair and darkness in our minds and hearts.

Because Christ has been raised from the dead, we can be sure that death doesn't have the last word.

In the movie, Brooke finds her teacher Grace at a coffee shop off campus and begins to explain her feelings of uncertainty. She asks, "How do you keep it together in spite of the challenges of life?"

Grace gives her a one-word answer: "Jesus."

Mentioning the name of Jesus not only starts Brooke on the path of hope but starts Grace on the path of persecution. Scripture says, *"Salvation is found in no one else, for there is no other name under heaven given to mankind by which we must be saved" (Acts 4:12)*. This is why there is such a conflict when the name of Jesus is mentioned.

Without a doubt, no other name brings such controversy. Could this be due to the fact that the spiritual enemy of mankind doesn't want anyone having hope?

Jesus said, *"The thief comes only to steal and kill and destroy; I have come that they may have life, and have it to the full" (John 10:10)*.

The promise of this kind of life means that God wants you to have hope. Therefore, you can be sure that if you're feeling hopeless, the enemy (Satan)—not God—is behind those feelings. It's critical to break free from these thoughts and lift up your expectations: By believing in Jesus Christ, your best days are ahead of you.

QUESTIONS FOR DISCUSSION

1) Is it fair to blame God for the evil and suffering in the world? Why or why not?

2) Have you ever talked in depth to someone who was struggling with these issues? Please share about your experience.

3) What can we do to get better prepared to help others who are struggling with these questions?

FOLLOW UP

Try to encourage three people this week. They could be waiters at a restaurant, your fellow students, or even family members. This can be the start to a fresh approach of helping others.

Think about 1 Peter 3:15–16. These verses are important in understanding how to play your part in God's plan.

Pray and ask God to put others in your life who can encourage you in your walk with Christ.

Read chapter 1, "Man, Myth, Messiah," from the book *Man, Myth, Messiah*.

LESSON 2

UNDERSTANDING THE EVIDENCE

KEY VERSE

"But these are written that you may believe that Jesus is the Messiah, the Son of God, and that by believing you may have life in his name."
—John 20:31

MOVIE QUOTE

J. Warner Wallace: "I'm not a Christian because I was raised in a Christian home; I'm a Christian because it is evidentially true."

MOVIE CLIP

Lee Strobel on the witness stand.

WARM-UP QUESTIONS

1) Have you talked to someone who doubted Jesus existed?
2) What do you think is the connection between faith and evidence?

INTRODUCTION

A turning point in the movie is when Grace's lawyer, Tom Endler, recognizes that Jesus was actually a real person and the Gospels record the actual words He spoke. He was then given the book *Man, Myth, Messiah: Answering History's Greatest Question* and told, "You've got a lot of reading to do." Likewise, all Christians must remember that their faith is rooted in history. We need to study the evidence so we can clearly explain why we believe Jesus rose from the dead and spoke the words that lead to eternal life.

The evidence for the resurrection of Jesus is greater than for nearly any other historical event or person of that time. A majority of historians recognize several facts that lead to that conclusion. During a trial scene in the movie, Lee Strobel, who is Professor of Christian Thought at Houston Baptist University and the author of more than twenty books about Christianity, including *The Case for Christ*, lists several of these facts, including Jesus's death, burial, and appearances to His disciples after the resurrection. Lee also mentions that basic details of Jesus's life are confirmed by non-Christian historical sources as well as the historical accounts in Scripture. Therefore, these events are not just religious beliefs that must be accepted by faith; they are historical facts that we can confidently accept as true.

Lee Strobel and Detective J. Warner Wallace are not fictional characters. They appear as expert witnesses and reveal their personal stories and their journeys from atheism to faith. Though they both started to study the claims of Christianity as skeptics, the evidence eventually convinced them that Christianity is true. They came to recognize that Jesus rose from the dead and the Gospels represent reliable historical records. These facts changed the course of their lives.

Here is an overview of that evidence.

1. HE LIVED.

Breaking news: Jesus lived!

The existence of Jesus in history is irrefutable. The evidence is so overwhelming that virtually all historians would recognize this fact. The only place where this is challenged is in the murky online world of Internet skeptics. At times, even atheists like Richard Dawkins (a biologist, not an historian) have made statements like "Jesus . . . if He even existed." But even Dawkins has since recanted and admits that Jesus lived. It's important to remember that being an expert in *one* area doesn't make you an expert in *all* areas.

This issue is raised in the movie when the statement is made about Jesus "allegedly" existing. This insinuation leads to Tom, Grace's attorney, calling for these expert witnesses to establish the fact that Jesus did indeed exist. It's understandable why skeptics attempt to challenge this fact. If you can cast doubt on the existence of Jesus, you have an easier time dismissing His words and moral authority in your life. Facts are pesky things. They tend to make a mark that isn't easily erased.

The evidence for the existence of Jesus is not only affirmed through the reliable historical records in Scripture but by other sources as well. In this lesson we will talk about people like the Jewish historian Flavius Josephus, who wrote during the time of Jesus. He was writing on behalf of Rome and was not sympathetic to Christianity. We will mention what he said in a moment. There were other historians and writers as well, including Tacitus and Pliny, who spoke about Jesus and established His existence in history.

It's important to remember that historians determine the validity of an event or a person's existence usually based on one or two sources. Many times these sources were written long after the event took place or the person lived. The fact that there are several ancient sources, along with the witness of the Gospels, makes the existence of Jesus of Nazareth a part of the historical bedrock.

As one skeptical historian concluded, "Jesus existed. And those who deny it do so, not because they have examined the evidence with the eye of an historian, but they have an agenda that this denial serves."

And as Lee Strobel says in the movie, "Denying the existence of Jesus doesn't make Him go away. It merely proves that no amount of evidence will convince you."

2. HE DIED.

The cross is the symbol of the Christian faith and without question the most recognizable emblem in the world. Almost two billion people believe that Jesus's crucifixion had something to do with their sins being forgiven by God. His death by crucifixion is well attested by history. It too is a part of the historical bedrock. The first-century historian Josephus wrote,

> *When Pilate upon hearing him accused by men of the highest standing among us, condemned him to be crucified. (Antiquities 18.63-64)*

The crucifixion is also attested by Tacitus, who is generally regarded as the greatest of the Roman historians. He was the proconsul of Asia from AD 112–113. *The Annals*, Tacitus's last work, was written around AD 116–117 and included,

> *Nero fastened the guilt [of the burning of Rome] and inflicted the most exquisite tortures on a class hated for their abominations, called Christians by the populace. Christus, from whom the name had its origin, suffered the extreme penalty during the reign of Tiberius at the hands of one of our procurators, Pontius Pilatus. (Annals 15.44)*

There are other ancient sources that we could mention, but these examples are sufficient to establish this fact in history. In addition, all four Gospels (each counts as an independent, reliable source) record the fact that Jesus was crucified. Paul the apostle, whom historians acknowledged as a real person, also wrote about the cross of Christ and its centrality to our faith.

Looking beyond the actual event of Christ being crucified and examining the meaning behind this act yields a life-changing message. As Paul later wrote, approximately twenty years after the crucifixion, "*For what I received I passed on to you as of first importance: that Christ died for our sins according to the Scriptures, that he was buried, that he was raised on the third day according to the Scriptures" (1 Corinthians 15:3–4)*. Christ's death was in fulfillment of the words of the prophets. The most significant of these was the prophet Isaiah, who wrote almost six hundred years before Christ:

> *Surely he took up our pain*
> *and bore our suffering,*

yet we considered him punished by God,
stricken by him, and afflicted.
But he was pierced for our transgressions,
he was crushed for our iniquities;
the punishment that brought us peace was on him,
and by his wounds we are healed. (Isaiah 53:4–5)

His death paid the price for our sins and provided the healing that we need for our broken spiritual condition. Through His death we can have life.

3. HE ROSE AGAIN.

The most significant fact recognized even by skeptics is that Jesus's disciples *believed* that they encountered Him after He rose from the dead. No other conclusion could explain what would have brought such a sudden and dramatic transformation in His followers. After Jesus was arrested, His disciples initially denied (Matthew 26:70) or abandoned Him (Mark 14:50). Shortly afterward, they boldly declared to hostile audiences—in the very city where the events had taken place—that they had encountered the risen Jesus.

In addition, the first witnesses of the resurrection were the women who initially discovered the empty tomb. Their testimony is significant since the testimony of women at that time was not even accepted in a court of law. No one would have chosen them to establish the truth of the story. The fact of the empty tomb is also significant since it indicates that the disciples did not encounter Jesus's spirit, which had left His body, but a physical Jesus with a resurrected body.

Jesus not only appeared to His followers, but He also appeared to two prominent skeptics. James, the half brother of Jesus, initially doubted Jesus's claims (Mark 3:21) but later became a leader of the Church. The reason for this dramatic change of heart? He saw Jesus alive after He had been raised from the dead. And Saul of Tarsus, the man who initially persecuted the early Christians, became a follower of Christ. Jesus appeared to him on the road to Damascus and appointed him as an ambassador to the Gentiles. In his letter to the church in Corinth, Paul (Saul) described Jesus appearing to Peter, the other disciples, James, himself, and five hundred others, many of whom were still alive (1 Corinthians 15:5–8).

The best explanation for the described facts is that Jesus actually rose from the dead. Skeptics have argued that the disciples made up the stories, but no motivation exists for such deliberate deception. What could possibly have caused these followers to initially flee for their lives and then conspire to make up the resurrection? Some of the disciples were sentenced to death for preaching the resurrection, yet none recanted to save his life. Many have died for believing something to be true, but no one dies for a story they know is a lie. In addition, a conspiracy by the disciples or a "group hallucination" (which is unprecedented) could not explain the appearances to James and Paul. Other equally implausible alternative explanations have been presented, but none can withstand even the slightest scrutiny.

4. HE IS LORD.

The resurrection of Jesus verified His identity as the Son of God. This means that He is not only the ultimate spokesperson for God but God Himself manifested in human flesh. As Paul wrote, *"And who through the Spirit of holiness was appointed the Son of God in power by his resurrection from the dead: Jesus Christ our Lord" (Romans 1:4).*

I've met people who have actually told me they were God. I usually respond and say, "If you're God, I've got a lot of questions for you." Of course they are delusional. Jesus was not like these kinds of people. His miracles were astounding and undeniable. He came in fulfillment of the Hebrew prophets who spoke of the coming Savior and Messiah. The ultimate proof was the fact that after He had died the horrible death of crucifixion through the hands of the Romans, He was alive again in three days. This verified *He was who He said He was.*

This is the ultimate mystery of the Gospel. God became man in Jesus Christ. He was not just a great prophet or teacher. Every prophet prefaced their words with the phrase "This is what the LORD says." But Jesus didn't say that. He said, "Very truly I tell you." He said things like *"I am the light of the world" (John 8:12)* and *"Heaven and earth will pass away, but my words will never pass away" (Matthew 24:35).* These are not the words of a mere man.

The fact that Jesus is Lord means He has the right to direct every area of our lives. Many look to Jesus as a counselor or consultant, but He has called us to make His teachings and commands our highest priority. In fact, He taught His followers, *"Whoever wants to be my disciple must deny themselves and take up their cross and follow me. For whoever wants to save their life will lose it, but whoever loses their life for me and for the gospel will save it" (Mark 8:34–35)*. The Christian faith does not work for many because they wish to fit Jesus into their lives instead of fitting their lives into Jesus's mission.

Even beyond, Jesus is Lord over all creation. Mark used the term "gospel" to describe Jesus's birth in the same way that pagan historians used it to describe the birth of the emperor Augustus Caesar. Mark and the other New Testament writers recognized that His words carried authority over all political rulers and powers. Therefore, we as Christians can boldly declare Jesus as Lord and Savior to all people.

5. HIS WORDS ARE TRUE.

The fact that Jesus is the resurrected Lord means that the words He spoke are the very words of God. Jesus was called *"the Word"* by the apostle John *(John 1:1)*.

When Jesus spoke, His words carried ultimate authority. The wind and sea obeyed His commands. Even His own disciples would say, *"No one ever spoke the way this man does" (John 7:46)*. Realizing that Jesus really lived and was crucified and raised from the dead on our behalf means that, as His followers, we treat His words with the ultimate respect and honor. We can also trust that God would have ensured His words were accurately recorded and preserved for future generations.

It's important to know that even though we have cited sources outside the New Testament to support such facts as the existence of Jesus, His death, and the empty tomb, we are in no way dismissing the reliability and authority of the Bible. Some skeptics argue that we can't use the Bible to defend the truth of our faith because the people who wrote it were believers and therefore biased. That is like saying if you're an American, you cannot be trusted to write a fair history of the United States.

The Bible is not one book, but a collection of books. The New Testament includes twenty-seven documents written by at least eight different authors. These writings are the best source for our knowledge about Jesus Christ. They not only attest to what others in history have claimed, but they also provide much more extensive details. Moreover, they explain the meaning and significance of the recorded events. And these writings have been shown to be accurate by enormous amounts of historical and archeological evidence.

In the court scene in the movie, J. Warner Wallace describes just a few of the many pieces of evidence that prove the reliability of the Gospels. In particular, the similarities and differences between the accounts of the Gospel writers perfectly match what would be expected of independent eyewitnesses accurately describing what actually happened. In addition, the authors wrote too recently after Jesus's ministry to have distorted the events. The Gospels also contain details that were embarrassing to the early church. For instance, they all describe the disciples misunderstanding Jesus's teaching and abandoning or denying Him after He was arrested. No author would have made up such embarrassing stories unless they actually happened. In addition, numerous historical discoveries have confirmed even minor details in the Gospels and the book of Acts, such as names of rulers, cultural practices, and historical events. In summary, no competent historian would doubt that the New Testament accurately describes Jesus's teaching and ministry unless that scholar assumed it was unreliable from the beginning.

QUESTIONS FOR DISCUSSION

1) Were you surprised that historians verified Jesus's existence outside of what was written in Scripture? Why or why not?

2) How does the resurrection verify that Jesus Christ is the true path to the Father?

3) Do you now have greater confidence that the Christian story is true? Please explain your answer.

FOLLOW UP

Read 1 Corinthians 15:3–8. This passage is acknowledged as an early creed that outlines the basic evidence of the Christian faith. To whom did Jesus appear? Why are these witnesses significant in giving us confidence that the resurrection really happened? Could Paul's readers confirm that he was telling the truth? How?

Ask the Holy Spirit to show you areas where His words have not been obeyed in your life. Recognize that to believe in Him as Lord and Messiah means to obey Him.

Read chapter 2, "The Minimal Facts," from *Man, Myth, Messiah.*

LESSON 3

PASSING THE TEST

KEY VERSES

"Consider it pure joy, my brothers and sisters, whenever you face trials of many kinds, because you know that the testing of your faith produces perseverance. Let perseverance finish its work so that you may be mature and complete, not lacking anything." —James 1:2–4

MOVIE QUOTE

Grace Wesley: "I'd rather stand with God and be judged by the world than stand with the world and be judged by God."

MOVIE CLIP

Grace in front of the school board. She refuses to apologize for what she did in the class and then explains to her lawyer why she can't compromise.

WARM-UP QUESTIONS

1) What has been the biggest test in your life?

2) Have you ever failed so badly you got to take a retest?

INTRODUCTION

Let's face it—everyone wants to be liked. From our pictures and posts online to the unique quirks of our personalities, we deeply care about our reputations. No one wants to be teased or ridiculed. Growing up with the first name *Rice* put me at the center of attention in a negative way at times when it came to being picked on. My worst nightmare would have been to be singled out about anything, especially my religious faith. This perspective changed when I became a follower of Christ. No longer was I as concerned with my own reputation; instead, I cared about the honor and respect given to the name of Jesus.

My commitment cost me many friendships. People were surprised that I didn't want to participate in parties and gatherings that I had usually attended. They weren't comfortable with me because I wanted to talk about the Lord and His love for them. I wanted to share my faith with everyone and see my school turned upside down for Christ. I became a new creation in Christ as the Bible promises (2 Corinthians 5:17). I'm so thankful for the people who helped me lay a solid foundation that emphasized repentance as well as faith and Jesus being Lord, not just Savior. They told me that being a Christian meant picking up my own cross and following Jesus. Included in that meant surrendering my pride and my fear of losing my reputation. In Romans 12:1, the apostle Paul called this being a *"living sacrifice"* and referred to it as our *"true and proper worship"* as authentic believers.

You probably know that people are being persecuted around the world for their faith. We have seen the images of believers wearing orange fatigues as members of ISIS hover over them, ready to execute them for being Christians. Our faith is rarely put to this kind of test. For most of us, it is our reputation that is threatened.

Regardless of where we live or what we are facing, we must trust that as we stand for Christ in the face of persecution, we demonstrate to the world around us the greatness of the Gospel and how limitless the love of God is. This kind of love is greater than hate, fear, and bigotry. It's the kind of love that will never let us down.

1. YOUR FAITH WILL BE TESTED.

In the first *God's Not Dead* movie, a young freshman in college (Josh Wheaton) is challenged to defend his faith in front of the entire philosophy class. Some suggested that this type of challenge was not realistic. They said, "No atheists are that angry." Really? There were scores of posts, tweets, and e-mails from people recounting a similar challenge in their own lives from teachers who were hostile to the Christian faith.

Now in *God's Not Dead 2*, there are fewer voices discounting the plot and whether something like this could happen. In the news, stories abound of people being persecuted for any expression of faith in the public schools.

Besides that, almost every character in the movie is involved in some type of testing when it comes to their faith—even those who seemingly don't have any interest in faith. This shouldn't be a surprise. Virtually every person in Scripture encountered a test of faith at some level as well. There are several reasons for this. First of all, our faith is tested in order *for us* to discover whether it is actually real. It's not for God's benefit but ours. We seldom enjoy the tests that we experience, but they help us see our strengths and weaknesses. Think about it: Taking a math test isn't for the teacher's benefit but to help you see if you grasped the material.

Second, when our faith is tested, it *helps others* see that it is real. Make no mistake . . . if you're a believer, people are watching your responses to the challenges you face. Even those who claim they have no faith are wondering if those who say they do are authentic. When they observe your faithfulness under pressure, it's a convincing witness for many.

One of the major stumbling blocks to unbelievers accepting the Christian faith is the problem of hypocrisy. Before I became a believer, I fell back on the idea that all so-called Christians were hypocrites. It wasn't fair to blame *all* people of faith for the failures of a *few*. Yet, all I needed was to meet one person who fully lived for Christ to change my mind. This indeed happened to me!

Finally, the testing of our faith demonstrates that the kingdom of darkness and its power over mankind have been defeated by the sacrifice of Christ at the cross (Colossians 2:15). Almost from the beginning, when mankind fell due to the influence of the evil one, there was a promise made to rescue us and give us victory over this power. God promises that in spite of the tribulations we experience, we can overcome even as Christ overcame (John 16:33).

2. HAVE CONVICTIONS, NOT JUST OPINIONS.

Just about everyone has an opinion on religion or spiritual issues. But there is a huge difference between having an opinion and possessing a real conviction. Opinions can change and they have little power to shape your actions; convictions are held deeply and do not change due to peer pressure or the situation you are in.

Some truths that exist are universally true, regardless of public opinion. The writers of the Declaration of

Independence referred to these truths as "self-evident." These deep-seated truths formed a moral code for these writers to hold on to, and they were willing to risk everything to defend them against tyranny and oppression. America was created by the type of people who held to their convictions to the point of risking their lives rather than compromising those truths in the face of threats.

Our culture today promotes a new pledge of liberty and tolerance for all. The promoters of this hyper-tolerance say we should be equally accepting of all views and beliefs. Ironically, they refuse to be tolerant when it comes to the Christian faith. In the movie, Grace's attorney dramatically brings this point out in her trial. This is also illustrated in the beginning of the movie when Principal Kinney claims that the school values diversity and tolerance, but their policy does not extend to Grace talking about Jesus as an historical figure in the classroom. In reality, many are tolerant of Christians, as long as they do not claim their beliefs are actually true and binding for all people—in other words, as long as they have opinions, not convictions. Grace demonstrates she holds her faith as a true conviction since she is willing to lose everything in order to stay faithful to Jesus.

The original disciples of Jesus preached the Gospel and confronted their culture with the conviction that Christ had been raised from the dead and was Lord and God. They said things like "*We must obey God rather than human beings*" *(Acts 5:29)* when told to be silent. Many of them would eventually lose their lives rather than deny their convictions about Jesus and what He commanded them to do. Most of us will never be put to the ultimate test of losing our lives because of our faith. Yet we will all have to lose something, whether that is friends, job opportunities, or social standings. The world was turned upside down by the convictions of the first disciples. We desperately need that type of faith today.

3. TAKE A STAND.

When you possess convictions, you will eventually have the opportunity to take a stand for those beliefs. "Taking a stand" is an expression that means you not only *stand up* for what you believe but you *speak up*, regardless of the consequences. To stand for something means you have determined that the values and beliefs you possess should not change, regardless of peer pressure or consequences. It requires courage and trust to voice a belief that might be unpopular or controversial. These kinds of convictions have been witnessed in great men and women of faith throughout history.

Not only do we stand firm in our convictions, we stand against the forces of darkness behind the scenes. As the apostle Paul wrote, *"Therefore put on the full armor of God, so that when the day of evil comes, you may be able to stand your ground, and after you have done everything, to stand" (Ephesians 6:13).* This means that we don't necessarily see people as our enemies, but we realize that we are battling against spiritual forces. These forces certainly influence people and wage war against us as believers. The pressure we feel to surrender our beliefs is definitely spiritual in nature and must be resisted. If we resist the devil, the Bible promises he will flee from us (James 4:7).

To stand also means to trust in God's promises in spite of the opposition. The very principles you stand for have promises attached to them. One of the things I heard as a new believer was the phrase "standing on the Word." (It doesn't mean to put your Bible on the floor and step on it.) This expression refers to holding on to the promises of God while you are facing trials and difficulties. One of the first examples for me was the promise found in 2 Timothy 1:7: *"For God has not given us a spirit of fear, but of power and of love and of a sound mind" (NKJV).*

Whenever I face a challenge of any kind, I still find comfort in that promise. God has made many other promises to be with us in trouble and to help us in our struggles. It is an ultimate expression of trust and faith to believe that God is working on our behalf in spite of the negative circumstances we face. I'm also comforted by the fact that the trials don't usually last very long. Though there are exceptions, most of them tend to be temporary and short lived. Regardless, we can have confidence that God is still with us, in both good times and bad.

4. KEEP CALM (AND CARRY ON).

As you have probably realized firsthand, standing for Christian truth often angers those who have embraced false or contrary beliefs—especially those who feel everyone is free to create their own morality. Biblical teaching also confronts many of the perspectives and values of modern society, so it will directly clash with many things taught in school and promoted in the media. As a result, many will respond unkindly to our message and especially to us personally when we hold to a biblical view of morality. When we are ridiculed or rejected, however, we should not speak from a posture of defiance or anger. Instead, our tone should be humble and gracious. We need to correct false beliefs gently and guide people to the truth thoughtfully.

A helpful approach to hostility is to ask *why* a person has become angry. Often, they are simply reacting against their false perceptions of Christianity. For instance, they may think the Bible teaches that God is harsh and unforgiving. Or they may believe Christianity requires people to follow arbitrary rules that prevent them from enjoying life. In such cases, you can correct their misunderstandings. For others, their anger comes from painful experiences with religion while growing up or unpleasant encounters with misguided Christians. We can convey remorse for their experiences but encourage them to explore the true Jesus as described in the Gospels.

Of course, many respond with hostility because they do not want Christianity to be true. They recognize that they are living in opposition to God's standards, so they wish to deny any possibility they will eventually stand before this Creator to give an account of their lives. Speaking the truth to them plants a seed in their heart that can bear fruit at a later time. Their resistance may simply indicate that your words touched upon some significant issue in their heart.

In the movie, you see these types of tensions explode

into public protests over Grace's simple statements about Jesus. She makes no disparaging remarks about anyone nor any statements condemning anyone else's beliefs or actions. There are no statements calling Jesus "Lord" or "Messiah" or any other religious designation that reveal her views about who Jesus really is. It is important to not return evil for evil or insult for insult. Regardless of why people respond in anger, we can demonstrate the character of Christ by not reacting with the same angry spirit.

5. FAILURE ISN'T FINAL.

Failing a test can be devastating—not just in school, but in these tests of our faith. As much as we want to encourage you to be prepared to pass the tests that will certainly come your way, you must also be prepared to handle failure if it should happen. This isn't intended to lower the expectations on us as believers but to build a defense against the voices of guilt and condemnation. Instead, we want to focus on the voice of the Holy Spirit encouraging us not to quit. To sin means to not just break God's commandments but to miss the mark in terms of His standards. This is the reason Jesus died on the cross: to pay the price for our sins and transgressions. Though we don't plan on sinning, we must have confidence in God and His promises concerning our opportunity to confess our sins, be forgiven, and try again.

This was one of the most important things I learned as a new believer. Someone told me, "Don't run *from* God when you sin, run *to* Him." Just like in the Garden of Eden, when Adam and Eve sinned, we all are tempted to hide from God or from those who are His followers. Yet God is merciful and patient with us. One of the great promises in Scripture is, *"If we confess our sins, he is faithful and just and will forgive us our sins and purify us from all unrighteousness" (1 John 1:9)*. If God can't use anyone who has ever failed, that would eliminate the entire human race! Looking back on my life as a believer, God has been merciful to me time and time again. Knowing that God is merciful hasn't resulted in me thinking that sin is no big deal. On the contrary, God's grace has produced a passion to honor Him by keeping His commands and faithfully standing for His Word.

This may be hard to believe, but many times our greatest victories come after we have had major failures. This was certainly the case for Peter, who failed his big test and denied knowing the Lord. He had boldly announced that even if all the other disciples denied Jesus, he would not. His failure was so public that we are still talking about it two thousand years later. Thankfully, Peter's failure wasn't the end of the story. Jesus forgave and restored him, and within sixty days of his great collapse, Peter preached a monumental message on the day of Pentecost and three thousand people believed and were baptized. The Gospel is not only good news for unbelievers, it is good news for believers that His love never fails.

QUESTIONS FOR DISCUSSION

1) Why is it important that your faith is tested?

2) What do you think about the way Grace was treated by the school board in the movie?

3) Have you ever faced any kind of persecution for your faith?

FOLLOW UP

If you are going through a tough time, ask someone to pray with you for strength. Remember, God gives grace to the humble. Though we feel vulnerable admitting our struggles, God promises to give us grace when we have an attitude of humility.

The next time you go to the gym to work out, reflect on how the weights you lift and the miles you run make you stronger physically. Do you see the connection between this and the struggles we encounter in life?

Read 2 Corinthians 4:7–18. The apostle Paul gives us his perspective on the struggles he has faced. How does he describe all the troubles he has experienced? (Hint: See verse 17.)

Read chapter 9, "Following Jesus," from *Man, Myth, Messiah.*

LESSON 4

SPREADING THE NEWS

KEY VERSE

"But in your hearts revere Christ as Lord. Always be prepared to give an answer to everyone who asks you to give the reason for the hope that you have. But do this with gentleness and respect." —1 Peter 3:15

MOVIE QUOTE

Grace to Brooke at the end of the trial: "Go spread the good news."

MOVIE CLIP

Martin sharing the Gospel with Brooke in church.

WARM-UP QUESTIONS

1) What was your favorite part of the movie?
2) Do you think you could have done what Grace did (taking the stand she took)?

INTRODUCTION

As we talked about in the last lesson, the Gospel isn't just good news for unbelievers but for believers as well. Jesus Christ offers us forgiveness and hope regardless of our sins and failures. A big part of that good news is that we are transformed as followers of Christ and can overcome the sin that can easily entangle us (Hebrews 12:1–2). Christianity isn't about managing a cycle of failure but learning that, in Christ, we can be "*more than conquerors through him who loved us*" *(Romans 8:37)*. This is the spirit of victory that lives inside of us as believers. Because it is the same Spirit that raised Christ from the dead, He can raise us up from any failure or sin that may have defeated us in the past. That's why it's important to say, *Failure isn't final!*

If we fully understand the Gospel ourselves, this becomes possible. That's why this final lesson is dedicated to us grasping the truth and power of this good news. As we mentioned in the beginning of this study, one of the major motivations for the *God's Not Dead* movies and the books that helped inspire them (*God's Not Dead* and *Man, Myth, Messiah*) is the fact that young people in America have left the Christian faith in alarming numbers over the last decade. One of the key reasons is their growing doubt about whether the Gospel is really true. The goal of this study has been to give you the confidence that it is true and that it should be communicated to the whole world! If we *truly* believe, then we will *certainly* speak.

One of the encouraging themes in the film is that when people grasp the Gospel, they are willing and ready to communicate it to others. Martin comes to the place of faith because of the faithful ministry of Pastor Dave. He is transformed from a person plagued by doubts and questions to someone sharing the Gospel with Brooke and leading her to Christ. This event plays a part in him wanting to return to China and become a pastor. Brooke is told by Grace at the end of the film to "go spread the good news." Can you imagine the impact on your school if you and your friends would do the same thing? This is how movements are started that can change the world. Let's look at some of the important traits that demonstrate we believe the Gospel.

1. CERTAINTY

No one has total certainty about everything. Yet we can have enough certainty about the Gospel to know it is true. Fables and fairy tales usually begin with the phrase "once upon a time." There is no attempt to convince the reader that the story is true. When it comes to the Gospel, it's the opposite case. As we learned in lesson 2, it is grounded in history.

The events surrounding the birth, life, death, and resurrection of Jesus Christ are not just statements of religious faith but statements of history that can be tested. Like other events in history, we can establish by several tests the probability that they happened.

First, there is the existence of multiple witnesses. When it comes to the key facts about Jesus, this is satisfied. Beyond the reliable accounts of the four Gospel records, there are also other sources outside of Scripture that speak of these important events. This points to another historical test: witnesses that are independent.

Another test is the principle of embarrassment. The Gospel writers revealed embarrassing testimony concerning their doubts, sins, and cowardice. Comparing the Gospels to other ancient documents shows just how reliable these records are. We can be certain that the events recorded in the Gospels actually happened. We also can look at what historian Gary Habermas calls the "minimal facts" about Jesus Christ. These facts are so witnessed by historians that even skeptical scholars (not the ones on the Internet) will acknowledge they are true. This is the case with the crucifixion of Jesus, His honorable burial, His tomb found empty by a group of His women followers, His appearance to both followers and skeptics, and the early proclamation of the Gospel message. Christianity started in the place where it could have most easily been disproved—in Jerusalem, just days after Christ was crucified.

Looking at these historical facts, we use a form of reasoning called "deduction." This asks the question, "What is the best explanation of the facts we know?" Some have suggested that Jesus's disciples stole His body and then went out and proclaimed He had risen. This would have required them to keep this lie a secret and then go out and risk their lives for a falsehood. Countless people have given their lives for what they *believed to be true*. But there is no evidence of people giving their lives for what they *knew to be false*. Another proposed explanation is that the Romans or the religious leaders moved the body. This is obviously false. All they would have had to do was produce the dead body of Jesus, and Christianity would have died on the spot. Several other alternative explanations have been given, but they are all equally implausible. The best explanation of the facts is that Jesus Christ was raised from the dead three days after His death. This is what the early disciples believed, and that faith changed the world!

2. CLARITY

One of the most humorous and embarrassing things to watch on TV is "people on the street" interviews. Usually late-night comedy shows send out reporters to ask people questions that reveal their ignorance on matters of history or current events. I recently watched a segment where people were asked what year Columbus sailed to the Americas from Spain. The answers ranged from 1292 to the 1960s. It was actually shocking to hear how uninformed they were. If you asked the average believer to give a definition of the Gospel, you would get a wide range of answers as well.

In my doctoral research, my focus was on how to reverse the negative trend of people abandoning the faith. One of the most important things that can impact this is for Christians to learn a clear definition of the Gospel. When this happens, it becomes much easier to present it to others as well as retain its truth for yourself. It can be a difference maker if you simply memorize and master a definition such as this:

> *The Gospel is the good news that God became man in Jesus Christ. He lived the life we should have lived and died the death we should have died . . . in our place. Three days later He rose from the dead, proving He is the Son of God and offering salvation and forgiveness of sins to everyone who repents and believes in Him.*

Breaking this down line by line will give you a greater comprehension of the life-changing aspects of the message.

God became man in Jesus Christ.

Jesus was not just a man, but the Creator of the universe in human form. His words were no ordinary words, and His miracles demonstrated His divine authority.

He lived the life we should have lived and died the death we should have died . . . in our place.
Christ's sinless life qualified Him to be the spotless offering for sin that the Law required. John the Baptist introduced Jesus as *"the Lamb of God, who takes away the sin of the world!" (John 1:29)*. He paid the price for our sins at the cross.

Three days later He rose from the dead, proving He is the Son of God.
His resurrection validated His identity as the Son of God, the promised Savior and Messiah.

[He offers] salvation and forgiveness of sins to everyone who repents and believes in Him.
We can receive a new life in Christ as we turn from our sins (repent) and put our faith in Christ. By trusting in Him we can see the penalty and guilt of our sins removed.

By committing this definition to memory, you will be prepared to clearly communicate it to others.

3. CONVICTION

There is a popular expression floating around that goes like this: "Preach the Gospel, and if necessary, use words." This is like saying, "Feed the hungry, and if necessary, use food." Sharing the Gospel requires our using words. Jesus said to "*make disciples of all nations . . . teaching them to obey everything I have commanded you*" *(Matthew 28:19–20)*. The early

Christians risked their lives by preaching the Gospel. If they had kept their mouths closed and only performed acts of kindness or service, they would have certainly lived longer lives. Instead, they responded to the authorities who tried to silence them by saying, "*We cannot stop speaking about what we have seen and heard" (Acts 4:20, NASB).*

This doesn't mean that we are arrogant or disruptive in our communication. We are to follow social or company rules as much as we can and certainly discern the appropriate times to speak or not to speak. What this refers to is the reality that some will try to silence the Gospel from ever being mentioned or communicated. We must be prayerful to understand when the right moments arrive for the message of Christ to be proclaimed. And we must pray for the boldness to speak and not allow the fear of man to intimidate us into silence.

We must also learn the art of dialogue and asking questions when it comes to talking with others. This approach is called SALT: Start a conversation, Ask questions, Listen, and then Tell the story (the Gospel). It will allow you to engage others in a winsome and gracious way and minimize the awkwardness that can leave a bitter aftertaste in everyone's mouths. We have developed a free app called TheGodTest (thegodtest.org) to help guide you in learning to start conversations that lead to a presentation of this life-changing message of Jesus Christ.

Once you embrace the mandate to be part of spreading the Gospel, you will be amazed at how many doors God opens. As you prepare yourself to help others, the opportunities to share will be more frequent. This is just like Martin in the movie, who continually searched for answers that not only strengthened his faith but allowed him to help Brooke come to the place of faith as well.

4. COMPASSION

The love of God should be our driving motivation to share the message of Christ with others. We have all seen how ugly it can get when people are angry in their communication toward others. We often confuse our own anger and frustration toward others who are non-Christians with God's perspective toward them. Scripture says God is kind to ungrateful people (Luke 6:35). It tells us that we are to love our enemies, not just those who are our friends and family. This kind of love is disarming. There are very few barriers that God's love won't penetrate. Perhaps the most popular verse in all the Bible is John 3:16: "*For God so loved the world that he gave his one and only Son, that whoever believes in him shall not perish but have eternal life.*"

When we attempt to love people the way God loves them, it opens their hearts and minds to receive the Gospel message. We don't do this as some type of gimmick to try to manipulate people into believing. Love must be sincere. Therefore, God must change our hearts first. As we pray and read God's Word, we are transformed in our inner attitudes toward others. Because God has forgiven us, we have compassion toward others who need this forgiveness as well. When I think of what I was like before I knew the Lord and the ungodly things I did, I am instantly merciful toward others. Time and time again, by being kind to people who were not kind to me, I found this to be far more effective in getting their attention than any insult or angry words (which was how I used to respond).

Scripture says that we have been given "*the ministry of reconciliation*" *(2 Corinthians 5:18).* This means that we are called to bring healing to the wounds of racism, bigotry, and relational breakdown at all levels. If this is to happen, we must not be people who are unforgiving of others or gossipers or slanderers. If we live that way, we will effectively be disqualified from helping others. When we see ourselves as reconcilers, however, we bring hope to every situation. Even when we carry ourselves this way, we still might not be received and our helpful motives recognized. I have been rejected and insulted many times for simply trying to help others. But overall, when my motive is to bring God's love and healing to others, good things usually happen. As Scripture promises, "*Love never fails*" *(1 Corinthians 13:8).*

5. CONNECTION

As we mentioned in lesson 1, we are called into relationship with God and with others. No one can really succeed without the right people helping them and standing with them as they face challenges. Jesus surrounded Himself with a group of men and women who He hoped would stand with Him. At the time of His darkest hour before the cross, He asked them to pray with Him. If Jesus needed friends, so do we. I've heard it said, "Show me your friends and I'll show you your future." Who we are connected with as friends is very important. This is why the heart of God's plan is to build His Church. Jesus announced, *"I will build my church, and the gates of Hades will not overcome it" (Matthew 16:18).* We are called to be part of the Church in a practical way so that we can be encouraged and receive the teaching and correction we need to grow spiritually.

The benefits of being connected to others are too many for me to mention in this short lesson. Chances are you are reading this study because someone invited you to a small group study where the issues of faith brought up in the movie are being discussed. There's a good chance that many questions have been answered and a fresh commitment to Christ has been made by you or someone you invited. The first time I attended a gathering of believers in college, I was struck by how sincere and passionate they were in their efforts to be faithful to Christ. I was so used to thinking all believers were hypocrites that I felt a little disoriented being around people who were just the opposite. I quickly realized that I was the *real* hypocrite.

Through being part of a local church and being trained and equipped, you can become an authentic follower of Christ. As you humble yourself and allow others to help you and hold you accountable in your commitments to be faithful to Christ's Word, you will begin to grow strong in faith and in grace. The end result is that you will soon become an effective witness and defender of the faith. It's no accident that many important scenes in the movie happen in a church. Pastor Dave and his friend Reverend Jude are constantly involved in helping people navigate the various crises they encounter. The church is indeed a place where many great things have happened to me. In turn, these encounters have led me outside the walls of the church and into a multitude of conversations and situations that desperately needed God's wisdom and His help.

This is the task He is calling us to. The greatest privilege in life is to partner with God in His work to redeem and rescue mankind. It all starts by answering the great question Jesus is asking you: "*Who do you say I am*?" *(Matthew 16:15).* Your answer to that question will be the most life-defining words you will ever speak.

The movie *God's Not Dead 2* portrays this truth in a dramatic way at the conclusion of the trial. Grace risks losing her job and her reputation because of her answer to this question. The kind of courage and faith she shows is what we need in real life from the millions who claim to be followers of Christ. Making the decision to live out the implications of the answer to that "great question" is really the first step you take to change the world.

QUESTIONS FOR DISCUSSION

1) Have you ever shared the Gospel with someone?

2) How has this study encouraged you to get involved in helping others?

3) How can we begin reaching out to our friends and fellow students?

FOLLOW UP

Copy the definition of the Gospel given in this lesson and commit it to memory.

Have someone hold you accountable to repeat it to someone else (from memory) at least once in the next week.

Read Romans 1. How many times does the apostle Paul mention the "gospel"?

Download TheGodTest app on your smartphone. See how easy it is to start conversations that can lead to sharing the Gospel using this tool.

Rice Broocks is the author of *God's Not Dead: Evidence for God in an Age of Uncertainty* and *Man, Myth, Messiah: Answering History's Greatest Question.* Rice is the cofounder of the Every Nation family of churches, which currently has more than one thousand churches and hundreds of campus ministries in more than sixty nations. He is also the senior minister of Bethel World Outreach Church in Nashville, Tennessee, a multiethnic, multisite church. Rice has a master's degree from Reformed Theological Seminary and a doctorate from Fuller Theological Seminary.

STUDENT STUDY LEADER'S GUIDE

PURE FLIX PRESENTS

A HAROLD CRONK FILM

GOD'S NOT DEAD 2

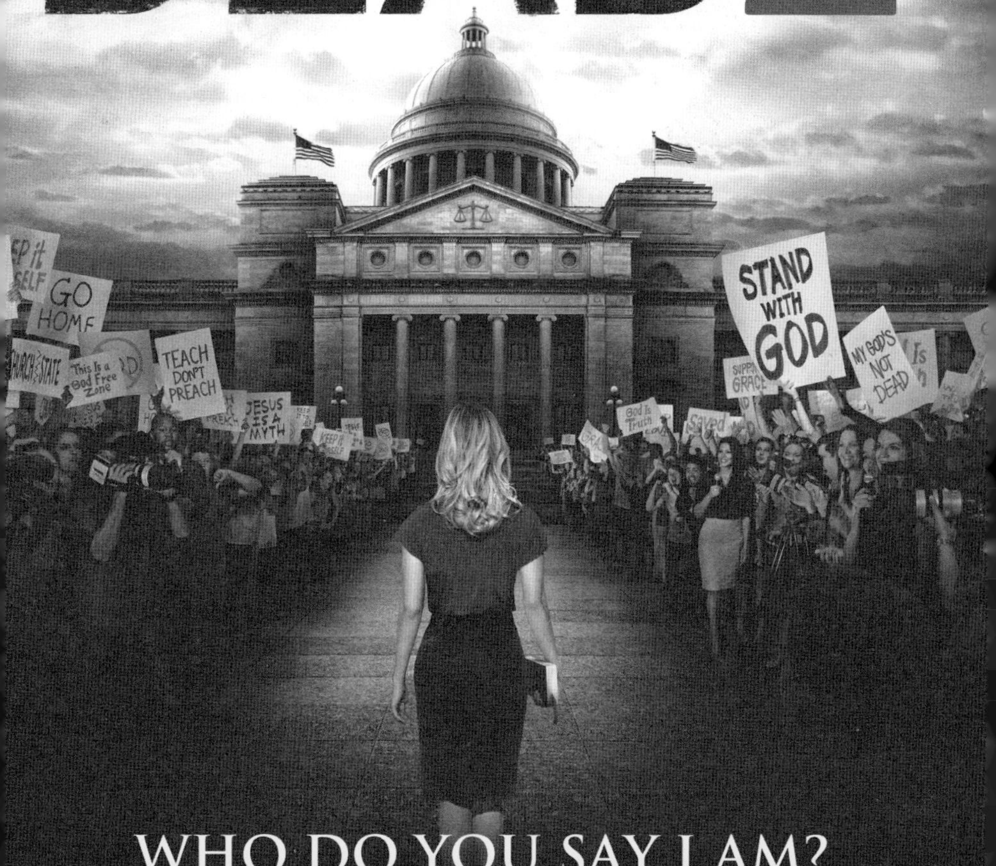

WHO DO YOU SAY I AM?

BY RICE BROOCKS

OUTREACH®

God's Not Dead 2: Who Do You Say I Am? Student Study Leader's Guide

Published by Outreach, Inc. Colorado Springs, CO 80919

www.Outreach.com

Cover and Interior Design by Alexia Garaventa
Written by Rice Broocks

Printed in the United States of America

INTRODUCTION: WHO DO YOU SAY I AM?

Rice Broocks

A few years ago, I wrote a book called *God's Not Dead: Evidence for God in an Age of Uncertainty*. I was deeply troubled by the reports of young people abandoning the Christian faith once they left high school and attended college. Studies showed they were being influenced by a rising chorus of skeptical voices from pop culture and vocal atheists claiming there was no evidence for God's existence. The goal of the book was to give a clear presentation of the evidence for God from science, philosophy, history, theology, and personal experience.

A friend of mine heard about the book I was writing and introduced me to Pure Flix, a faith-based movie company that expressed interest in bringing this drama to the big screen. They flew to Nashville, where I live, and we discussed the challenge that people of faith face on the university campus. It was deeply encouraging to hear their desire to do something that could give a response to the voices of atheism and unbelief and help people of all ages gain the solid footing needed for a real and lasting faith. It was an amazing thing to see those conversations and the evidence I was writing about turned into a movie called *God's Not Dead*. It became a box-office success in the United States and was shown literally around the world.

Even before the first movie was completed, there was discussion about another movie that would tackle the issue of the existence of the historical Jesus. I embarked on another writing journey on a book called *Man, Myth, Messiah: Answering History's Greatest Question*. It has resulted in the sequel, *God's Not Dead 2*. The story line is compelling, and the movie itself is based on true-to-life events and challenges that are happening in America with increased frequency and intensity.

It's becoming glaringly apparent that any reference to the Christian faith in the public square is unwelcome. This has had an enormous impact on the values and beliefs of an entire generation of young people. Although there are many theories that try to explain this decline, one of the primary reasons we have discovered is *they don't believe the Gospel story is really true.* This has less to do with the skeptics presenting real evidence against the truth of the Christian faith and more to do with the unfounded and untrue attacks hurled against believers to dissuade them with mockery and ridicule.

In many countries of the world, Christians are *assaulted* for their beliefs; in America, they are *insulted* out of their faith.

Our response? *Real faith isn't blind.* It is based on evidence, not merely subjective experience. Christianity answers the deepest questions of the heart *and* mind. Tragically, if those answers aren't known, it means there is no foundation that undergirds someone's faith. Merely having religious traditions isn't enough. I bet you have known people who seemed to be solid believers but were blown away when they faced intellectual challenges to their faith. As Scripture warns, *"My people are destroyed from lack of knowledge" (Hosea 4:6).*

While Bible studies and youth activities abound, there must be a clear understanding of the Gospel and an unwavering conviction of its truth. There is no way you can boldly live for Christ without a solid foundation that can withstand the challenges of skepticism and unbelief. In the movie *God's Not Dead 2*, a high school teacher, Grace Wesley, mentions Jesus Christ in a public classroom and then quotes His words written in the Gospels. She is suspended from her job and faces a lawsuit for her actions. Her crime? Simply referring to the words of the most influential person who ever lived. She finds herself having to take a stand, which could result in her losing her job. Her type of courage in the face of opposition is an inspiration to all of those who are being pushed, intimidated, and told to keep their faith locked up and far away from any public expression. Her boldness helps point people to the truths of the Gospel. This shouldn't just happen in the movies.

Our deepest desire is that through these *God's Not Dead* films, books, and study guides, there will be a multitude of believers who will become defenders of the faith and take the kind of stand Grace took. The story line of *God's Not Dead 2* includes a young girl named Brooke Thawley, who has lost her beloved brother and is searching for hope in the face of this family tragedy. Her parents are skeptics and simply want to "move on" rather than deal with the issues of eternity and life after death. Brooke's struggle leads her to her high school history teacher Grace Wesley, who shares her faith in Jesus with Brooke. This search for answers is a common theme in the movie.

Martin, the college student from China we met in the first movie, brings a list of 147 questions to Pastor Dave for answers.

Amy, the skeptical reporter from the first movie, discovers she's been healed from cancer and dedicates her writing to chronicle her search for God.

Grace, the high school teacher, is searching for the reasons why she is facing such persecution and why she feels abandoned by God in her struggle.

All of these types of struggles are common today as people search for answers to the pressing questions that arise from a dramatically shifting moral and political landscape. The real question now is: Whose words should we trust?

In the movie, Grace is called to the witness stand and asked to reveal how God had actually spoken to her. She reluctantly explains how she believes God asked her a question through a church sign she encountered: "Who do you say I am?" I call this "history's greatest question" in the book *Man, Myth, Messiah.*

Answering this question will be the defining decision of every person's life: Was Jesus a man, a myth, or the Messiah?

If He was just a man, we can admire Him.

If He was a myth, we can be entertained and even inspired by these heroic tales just as we are when we watch *The Avengers* or some other super hero story.

But if He is the Messiah, that means we should follow Him with all our heart, soul, mind, and strength. It also means that His words are the ones we can trust.

If there is no clear moral authority, then we are left with the schoolyard challenge, "Says who?"

The loss of faith we have described has left masses of people searching for meaning and purpose like never before. It is impossible to ignore the spiritual hunger in the human soul. In fact, people will eat whatever they can find to try to meet this need. Eventually people will eat dirt if they get hungry enough.

This presents us with an unprecedented opportunity to share the truth and hope that Christ offers. Tragically, at the time when hearts and minds are most open to look again to God for answers, God's people are not prepared to take advantage of this massive need. It is our prayer that through this study, each participant will come to the place of confidence in answering the great question the way Grace does in the movie: *"You are the Messiah, the Son of the living God" (Matthew 16:16).*

—Rice Broocks

GETTING STARTED

Thank you for choosing the *God's Not Dead 2: Who Do You Say I Am?* DVD-Based Study. Our prayer is that in the next four weeks, you and your group members will:

- Develop a better understanding of who Jesus is
- Go deeper in your relationship with Jesus
- Acquire a firm foundation on which to defend your faith in the midst of opposition

This small-group leader's guide will focus your attention on the DVD-based study, the resources inside the kit, and how to use them successfully.

Below are steps you can take to have a successful group experience with *God's Not Dead 2*.

STEPS FOR SUCCESS

1. READ THIS SMALL-GROUP LEADER'S GUIDE.

It will give you an overview of *God's Not Dead 2* and provide guidance for leading discussions with your group. This guide includes information on the themes in the movie and how you can use the film with this study.

2. REVIEW THE *GOD'S NOT DEAD 2 STUDENT STUDY GUIDE.*

Review the study guide to become familiar with each week's small-group study and discussion questions.

3. INVITE PEOPLE TO JOIN YOUR GROUP.

Even if you already have an established group with plenty of members, *God's Not Dead 2* provides you with an opportunity to invite other people to join you. There are many in your community who are searching for joy and purpose in their lives, but they don't know the truth about Jesus Christ.

Prayerfully consider whom you might invite to join your *God's Not Dead 2* DVD-Based Study and encourage your current members to do the same. Your invitations could make an eternal difference!

4. COMMUNICATE WITH YOUR GROUP MEMBERS.

Contact your group members to let them know when your meetings will start and what to expect. Determine whether your church is providing a *God's Not Dead 2 Student Study Guide* for each small-group member, if you're going to purchase the book for your members and have them reimburse you, or whether your members will purchase the study guide on their own.

Once you begin your sessions, communicate with your members every week to encourage them, remind them of weekly insights, and provide prayer and support.

GOD'S NOT DEAD 2 STUDY GUIDE

The study guide is a key element in the overall study. It is designed to correspond and work with the *God's Not Dead 2* Student DVD-Based Study by teaching each person in your group important life lessons, both through your group discussion and with individual questions that follow each session.

The study guide was written to help participants discover answers to their questions about who God really is and learn how to defend their faith even in the midst of increasing opposition in our culture.

WHAT IS THE *GOD'S NOT DEAD 2* STUDY?

The *God's Not Dead 2* DVD-Based Study is a four-week study designed to help everyone—those who are new to the faith and those who have been believers for many years—discover what they believe, evidence for the existence of God, and how to defend their faith. Based on clips from the film *God's Not Dead 2,* the study includes everything you need to grow deeper in your relationship with God and have the courage to stand up for what you believe.

There are four themes covered:

- **SEARCHING FOR ANSWERS** – Pain and crisis produce a search for God.
- **UNDERSTANDING THE EVIDENCE** – The evidence for the historical Jesus.
- **PASSING THE TEST** – As believers, our faith is tested.
- **SPREADING THE NEWS** – Communicating the Gospel to others.

For all four there are discussion questions in the *God's Not Dead 2 Student Study Guide* to help your group go deeper into Scripture and into your relationship with God.

In this study you will:

- Discover the evidence for the existence of the historical Jesus
- Be able to answer skeptics who question Jesus's existence
- Gain a deeper faith based on the evidence and not merely personal experience
- Be emboldened to defend your faith in a culture that increasingly opposes Christianity in the public square

Finally, the life-changing benefit each participant will derive from this study will depend, in large part, on each individual's desire and determination to discover and put into practice the truths and insights they receive.

GUIDELINES FOR LEADING A SMALL GROUP OR CLASS

LEADERS CAST A VISION.

Leaders are critical to the success of any group. As a small-group or class leader, your enthusiasm and example can inspire your members to:

- Consistently attend group meetings
- Openly participate in discussions
- Faithfully complete individual lessons
- Draw closer to God
- Invite others to join your group

Pray for the requests shared by group members during the week. Cast a vision for your group! Those who follow you will rise only as high as the expectations you set, so cast a vision of complete participation.

LEADERS FOLLOW GOD.

"David said to the Philistine, 'You come against me with sword and spear and javelin, but I come against you in the name of the LORD Almighty, the God of the armies of Israel, whom you have defied.'" —1 Samuel 17:45

Leading a group can be time-consuming, but be sure to set aside enough quiet time for you to be strengthened and encouraged by God. The foundation for your leadership will come from the peace and wisdom you find in your own relationship with God.

LEADERS PRAY.

"As for me, far be it from me that I should sin against the LORD by failing to pray for you. And I will teach you the way that is good and right." —1 Samuel 12:23

Pray for guidance about who to invite to your group and for God to encourage their participation. Once your group begins, ask for prayer requests and encourage all of your members to pray for each other. God's mighty hand moves in response to our prayers!

LEADERS ENCOURAGE.

"In all my prayers for all of you, I always pray with joy because of your partnership in the gospel from the first day until now, being confident of this, that he who began a good work in you will carry it on to completion until the day of Christ Jesus." —Philippians 1:4–6

Encourage your members to come to each weekly session, be involved, pray, and complete the reading in the *God's Not Dead 2 Student Study Guide* so they will get the most out of this DVD-based study. Encourage them to be receptive to God continuing His work in them and in their families.

LEADERS INVITE AND INCLUDE.

"I have become all things to all people so that by all possible means I might save some." —1 Corinthians 9:22

The *God's Not Dead 2 Student Study Guide* is intended for both Christians and those who have not yet entered into a relationship with Christ. This study has the power to help group members experience God's amazing love for them and help them study God's Word. At the end of the four weeks, they will have been encouraged to draw closer to God and be inspired to stand up for their faith in any arena, even in the midst of opposition.

Pray for God to bring to your mind the names of people you can invite to your group. Be conscious of how to make new members feel comfortable and welcome at each session. Encourage your members to invite their friends and neighbors to join them in the group.

As you lead each session, be sensitive to personality types (for example, introvert and extrovert). Gently draw out quieter members by asking nonthreatening questions. Talkative members may need to be gently reminded to allow everyone to participate.

GUIDELINES FOR YOUR GROUP

During your first session, review group guidelines with your participants. See some suggested guidelines below. You can read these to your group, or write your own guidelines using these as a starting point.

- **Priority:** Make the group meeting a priority in your schedule. If you are unable to attend or are running late, contact the group leader.
- **Preparedness:** Prepare for the lesson each week and come ready to share. What you put into the lesson is what you'll get out of it.
- **Participation:** Participate in the discussion, but keep answers brief so others may share as well.
- **Respect:** Remember that everyone has a right to their opinion, and all questions are encouraged and respected. Listen attentively to others without interrupting them.
- **Confidentiality:** Anything of a personal nature that is said in the meeting should not be repeated outside the meeting. This group is intended to be a safe place for open discussion and sharing.

- **Honesty:** Strive to be real and honest as you share with the group. If you have suggestions about how to improve the group sessions, discuss them with the leader.

- **Connectedness:** Seek to know and care for other group members, as well as share transparently regarding your own emotional, spiritual, and physical needs.

- **Support:** Actively support the mission and values of the small group and refrain from gossip and criticism. Communicate directly and privately with anyone with whom you have an issue.

GUIDELINES

FORMAT AND SCHEDULE

The *God's Not Dead 2: Who Do You Say I Am?* DVD-Based Study is organized as described below.

INTRODUCTION

This gives some basic information on the study that will familiarize you and your group members with each of the sections of the study guide and their purpose.

GOD'S NOT DEAD 2 MOVIE

Going to see *God's Not Dead 2* together, or showing it in your church or youth group, is a great way to kick off a new small group, or a new session for your existing group. Even if some or all of the members of your group have seen the movie, watching it together will give you an opportunity to catch details you might have missed. And, seeing the film together is a great opening for a thought-provoking discussion on what's really valuable in life.

SMALL-GROUP SESSION

During your weekly study, your group will watch the video clip for that week's theme. This is located on the Resource DVD in the DVD-Based Study Kit. Your group will then open the *God's Not Dead 2 Student Study Guide,* so you'll want group members to bring their own guides and turn to that week's session.

You will all read the Scripture passage and answer some questions relating to the short video clip you just watched from *God's Not Dead 2,* so encourage your group members to pay close attention during each weekly video session. There will also be a series of questions designed to engage your group with the principles of that week's Bible study.

Also, during the sessions, encourage members to share what they have been learning from the discussion sessions and how God has been speaking to their hearts about what they've read and studied that week.

Remember that the DVD-based study should help each of your group members seek God and discover great truths from God's Word. Your small group will help members dig deeper into the topic for that week, and the video will help illustrate the concepts being studied.

SESSION TIMING

Each weekly session is designed to be approximately ninety minutes. The length of the session will vary depending on the level of group participation and how well the discussion stays focused.

You can manage your group by encouraging everyone to participate in the discussions, but also by reminding them to keep their answers brief to allow everyone a chance to contribute. Keep the discussion focused on the topic and on the specific question the group is addressing. Small-group meetings are a great time to share conversation and build friendships, but you can arrange for snacks and social time after the group discussion is completed. If the conversation strays to other topics, gently redirect the group back to the guide's small-group study and discussion questions.

NOTES